**At play . . .**

Laughter can quickly turn to tears if someone falls on broken glass, or tumbles out of a tree.

**In the street . . .**

Stepping off the pavement or crossing the road without looking gives drivers no chance of avoiding an accident. Know your Green Cross Code, and use it!

**On the roads . . .**

Children riding bicycles must take special care, for many accidents happen on the roads. A bicycle should be the correct size for its rider, otherwise it cannot be ridden safely. Brakes, handlebars, lights, etc., should be checked regularly by a grown-up.

Some accidents cannot be avoided. This is where First Aid comes in — knowing what to do when someone is hurt.

# Contents

First edition

# First steps in
# First Aid

by IAN ROY

with illustrations by
DRURY LANE STUDIOS

Ladybird Books  Loughborough

## DOING WHAT YOU CAN

Although it's very easy to have an accident, it's surprising how many people know nothing at all about First Aid. They're unable to help, and may even panic because they don't know how to cope with the sudden emergency.

Yet First Aid is only doing what you can immediately after an accident happens. This book will show you some of the simple actions you can take to prevent further injury, ease pain and even, in very serious cases, keep someone alive.

Just as important, you will find out what NOT to do. Doing the wrong thing can often make matters worse, or cause more pain.

When you're dealing with an emergency, remember these three steps:

AT ONCE
> Give the First Aid which will prevent an injury from becoming worse.

**AS SOON AS POSSIBLE**
Get grown-up help.

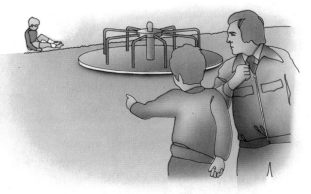

**THEN**
Make your patient comfortable.

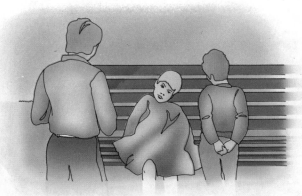

Many everyday injuries, however, are quite simple and can be easily treated. This book will also tell you how to look after them.

## WHAT'S WRONG?

You can't help someone who has been hurt until you find out what's wrong. Be a First Aid Detective. Look for clues. Fit them together like the pieces of a jigsaw puzzle to discover what help is needed. Remember, too, that there may be more than one injury.

There are three ways to find out what's wrong:

HISTORY

Ask what happened. Your patient may tell you: "I fell off my bicycle." Someone who saw the accident might say that he struck his head and fell on to his right arm. This kind of information is called the *history*.

## SIGNS

Use your eyes and hands to discover signs of injury. Is your patient's face pale or flushed? Does his skin feel cold and sweaty, or hot and dry? Is there any blood, bruising or swelling? These are all *signs*.

## SYMPTOMS

Ask your patient if anything *feels* wrong. Only he will be able to tell you that. He might say: "I can't move my leg," or perhaps: "I'm feeling sick." These are *symptoms*.

When you have found out what's wrong, you will then be able to give First Aid.

## ABOUT THE BODY
## 1 BREATHING

The body must have oxygen for life. Every minute we breathe in about sixteen times, drawing air, which contains the oxygen we need, into our lungs.

Here the air mixes with blood pumped from the heart. The blood takes in oxygen, returns to the heart, and is pumped all over the body. The body then uses the oxygen as fuel, leaving a waste gas called carbon dioxide. This waste gas is replaced by life-giving oxygen when blood returns to the lungs.

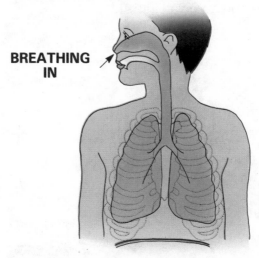

**BREATHING IN**

THE LUNGS

    The lungs are like two sponges, one on each side of the chest.

*Breathing in* draws air through the nose or mouth, down an airway into the lungs. The lungs expand and the air, containing oxygen, mixes with the blood.

*Breathing out* squeezes the lungs. This forces the air, now containing waste carbon dioxide, back up the airway and out through the nose or mouth.

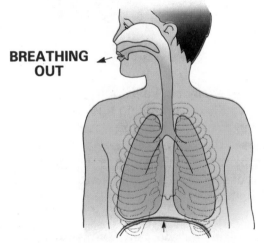

**BREATHING OUT**

If you have been running hard, you use up more energy and need more oxygen. Because of this, you breathe more often, and more deeply. Sometimes you need so much oxygen that you gasp for breath. When resting or sleeping, you use far less oxygen, so you breathe more slowly. After an accident, sitting or lying down reduces the amount of energy the body needs, and helps it to cope with the injury.

## CHOKING

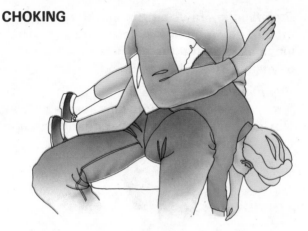

Someone can easily choke if food goes down "the wrong way", or something sticks in the throat. Air can't reach the lungs. Usually coughing clears the airway, but sometimes it is blocked completely. If this happens, coughing becomes impossible. Breathing is a struggle, and the face turns blue.

### Action

Help as quickly as you can. Bend your patient over the back of a chair, or get him down on to his hands and knees with his head lower than his chest. Slap him hard several times on the back, just below his shoulders. If this doesn't clear the airway, use your finger to hook out the object blocking his throat.

### DON'T

Don't waste time — every second counts.

## FAINTING

Fainting is caused by a brief shortage of blood supplying oxygen to the brain. It can happen when someone has been standing up for too long, has had a bad fright, or has been in a hot, stuffy room. He will feel weak and dizzy, and his face will be pale, cold and sweaty. A faint will last only a few minutes and is not serious.

### Action

**If your patient is feeling faint, sit him down with his head between his knees and his arms down by his legs. Tell him to breathe deeply. Loosen any tight clothing.**

**If he actually does faint, place him in the Recovery Position** *(see page 12)* **and loosen tight clothing. When he wakens and begins to feel better, you may give him sips of cold water.**

## UNCONSCIOUSNESS

When someone is unconscious, he looks asleep, but cannot be wakened. While he is like this he is in real danger of choking, especially if he is left lying on his back. His tongue could slip back into his throat, or he might be sick.

Many road accident victims die because they have choked while unconscious.

*The recovery position*

Look after an unconscious person by placing him in the Recovery Position, which is safe and comfortable. Follow these step-by-step instructions.

1 Loosen tight clothing at neck, chest and waist. Empty your patient's mouth. If he is wearing glasses, remove them.

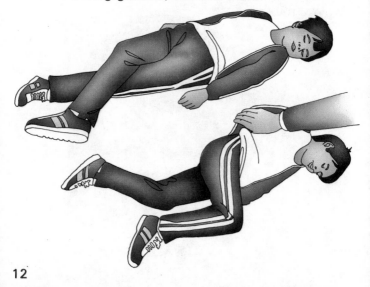

2 If the patient is lying on his back, kneel at his waist and tuck his arms close to his sides. Cross the leg furthest away from you over the other one.

3 Grasp his clothing at the hip and pull him towards you. Now pull his top leg up, so that the thigh is straight out from his body, and the knee is bent. Bend the other leg slightly at the knee.

4 Place the patient's upper arm so that his hand lies just in front of his face. Pull his lower arm slightly behind him. Tilt his head well back, with chin forward to keep the airway clear.

5 Cover him with a blanket to keep him warm.

**DON'T**

Don't try to move a patient if you think he may have broken bones in his neck or back.

## ABOUT THE BODY
## 2 CIRCULATION

*Oxygen, food and warmth*
Blood supplies the body with oxygen, food and warmth. It is sent throughout the body by the heart, which is really a strong muscle.

The heart beats about 60-80 times every minute

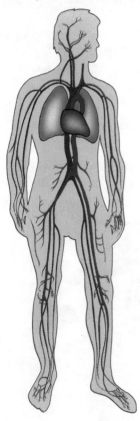

(about 100 times a minute in young children). Each time it beats, it pumps blood to all parts of the body through strong tubes called *arteries*.

*Feel the pulse*
You can easily feel this pulse beat. Put your fingertips on the inside of your wrist, below your thumb, where an artery lies close to the skin. Use only your fingers – your thumb has a pulse of its own.

The arteries divide again and again, getting smaller each time, until they become tiny capillary tubes reaching into all parts of the body.

This is where the life-giving oxygen is used up and replaced by waste carbon dioxide. The blood then flows back to the heart through veins. Blood containing oxygen is bright red. When it loses the oxygen, it becomes darker. This is why veins look blue.

*Slowing the pulse*
Very bad bleeding can be slowed by resting or lying down. This reduces the amount of oxygen the body needs, and the pulse slows. It is harder for the heart to pump blood upwards. To see this for yourself, hold one hand high in the air for a few minutes, then look at the backs of both hands. You will notice that the hand you have held up is paler, because less blood has been reaching it. Raising an arm or leg which has been cut helps to slow down bleeding.

## CUTS AND GRAZES

A wound is a cut or break in the skin which lets blood out, and germs in. Simple cuts and grazes usually stop bleeding by themselves after a few minutes, as the blood forms a clot to seal the wound.

**Action**

**Allow the blood to flow for a moment or two. This helps to clean dirt or germs away from the wound.**

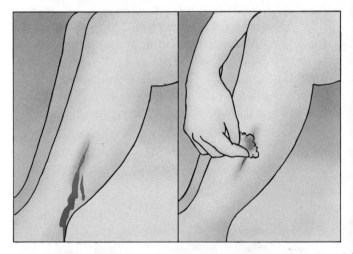

**Clean the skin around the wound by wiping gently with a small swab of cotton wool soaked in an antiseptic solution or warm soapy water. If using antiseptic solution, *read the instructions* on the bottle. Usually it must be diluted with water.**

Always wipe *away* from the wound. Use a clean piece of cotton wool for *each wipe*, otherwise you will only push more dirt and germs into the wound.

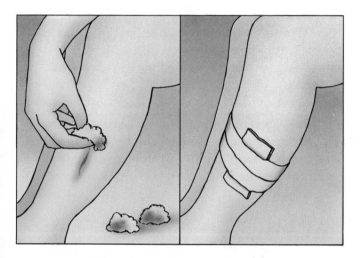

When you have cleaned the wound, apply an antiseptic cream and cover it completely with a gauze dressing. Keep this in place with a bandage or adhesive tape.

If the wound is large or dirty, or if grit is embedded under the skin, it should be treated by a doctor.

**DON'T**

Don't touch the wound with your fingers.

Don't touch the dressing – hold it carefully at the corners.

## BAD BLEEDING

Don't be afraid of bad bleeding. Blood can spurt or pour very quickly from a bad wound, and this can be very alarming. But it can often look worse than it really is.

Someone who loses a great deal of blood will suffer from *shock (see page 36)*, so it is important to stop bad bleeding as quickly as possible.

### Action

**Quickly make a pad from a gauze dressing, bandage, clean handkerchief or tea-towel. If using a handkerchief or tea-towel, unfold so that the cleaner inside surface is against the wound.**

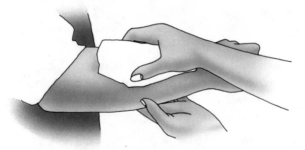

**Press the pad hard on the wound. If blood soaks through it, don't remove it. Cover with cotton wool or another pad, and keep pressing as hard as you can.**

**If you can't find a pad quickly and bleeding**

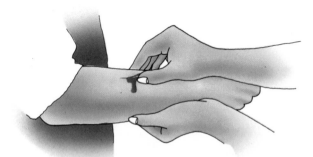

is really bad, don't waste time looking.
Press the *edges* of the wound together with
your fingers.

*Slow down the
pulse*
Lay your patient
on his back.
Raise an arm or
leg that is
bleeding badly,
unless it is
broken, and
continue to
apply pressure.

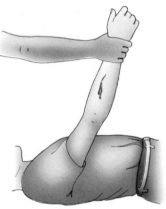

## DON'T

Don't touch a wound with your fingers.
Don't breathe over a wound.
Don't wipe off blood clots which may have
formed.
Don't use fluffy material for a pad, as fluff
will stick to the wound.

## NOSE BLEEDING

Bleeding from the nose is not usually serious, but can be worrying because of the amount of blood that is lost.

**Action**

Sit your patient down, bending slightly forward over a basin to catch drops of blood. Ask him to breathe through his mouth, and pinch the soft part of his nose below the bridge between his fingers and thumb.

**Make a cold compress. Press this over the bridge of his nose. The cold closes blood vessels in the nose, slowing down bleeding and making it easier to stop. Loosen tight clothing at neck and chest.**

*How to make a cold compress*

Make a pad from a handkerchief or cotton wool. Soak this in cold water, and squeeze it nearly dry.

**DON'T**

Don't tilt your patient's head back, as blood might flow into his throat and choke him.
Don't push cotton wool into his nose.
Don't allow him to blow his nose or disturb any clots which may have formed.

21

## BUMPS, BRUISES AND STRAINS

Bumps and bruises can be caused by a hard knock, and strains by over-stretching a muscle. Tiny blood vessels just below the skin are damaged. Blood leaking out of them spreads under the skin to cause swelling and often a bluish patch. The injury will be painful and tender to the touch.

### Action

Cool the bump, bruise or strain as quickly as you can to ease the pain and reduce the swelling. Gently but firmly, keep a cold compress or ice-bag on the injury for about half an hour. Make your patient comfortable. If the injury is in an arm or leg, raise it to slow down the blood supply. This will help to reduce swelling or bruising.

## *How to make an ice-bag*

Half-fill a polythene bag with crushed ice. Add a
little salt, squeeze out the air and seal the bag
shut. Wrap a thin cloth round the bag and hold it
gently over the bump or bruise.

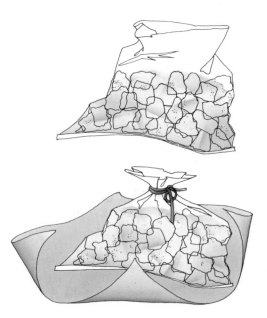

## *Trapped fingers*

A finger trapped in a door or between two hard
surfaces can become bruised under the nail.
Hold the finger in cold water or under the cold
tap for at least ten minutes. Then keep the
injured hand raised to reduce swelling.

## ABOUT THE BODY
## 3  NERVES

The nervous system keeps us aware of all that is happening around us. Without nerves, we would be unable to do anything. We would not be able to move, see, hear, feel or taste.

### A delicate computer

The brain is the "operations centre" of the body's nervous system. Like a delicate computer, it receives a continuous stream of messages from all over the body, and sends out instructions for the body to obey. These messages pass through a network of white threads called nerves, which keep the brain in touch with all parts of the body.

If you touch something hot or unpleasant, for instance, a nerve in your fingertip flashes a warning along the nerve. In a split second, the response comes back that tells your muscles to snatch your hand away.

When nerves are put out of action, there is a loss of feeling or movement in that part of the body.

### Communications cable

The nerve threads are gathered together into a communications cable, which runs to the brain through a tunnel in the spine. Damage to this spinal cord can result in permanent loss of movement to the whole body below the injury.

A SIMPLIFIED
DIAGRAM OF THE
NERVOUS SYSTEM
SHOWING THE
INCREDIBLE NETWORK
OF NERVES REACHING
OUT TO ALL PARTS
OF THE BODY FROM
THE BRAIN VIA
THE SPINAL CORD

## BURNS AND SCALDS

*Burns* are caused by dry heat. If you touch something very hot, like an iron or fire, you will burn yourself. *Scalds* come from wet heat, such as steam or boiling water.

As well as damaging the skin and nerve-endings, burns and scalds destroy blood vessels just below the surface.

A slight burn only turns the skin red. A more serious burn, however, forms blisters and the skin may even become charred or blackened. How serious a burn is, often depends on how much skin has been affected, not on how deep it is.

The First Aid for burns and scalds is the same.

### Action

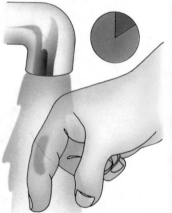

Cool a burn or scald at once. Don't waste time pulling off clothes. Gently, pour cold water over the injury, or hold it under the cold water tap. You can dip it into a basin or bath of cold water, or cover it with a cold, wet cloth.

*You must keep cooling it for at least ten minutes.*

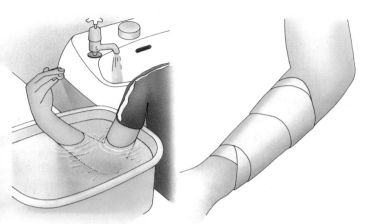

Cooling prevents further damage, eases the pain and helps to keep swelling down.

When the burn or scald has been cooled, gently remove anything tight near it, such as a watch, bracelet or ring. This will prevent more pain if the injury swells.

Cover the injury with a clean, *dry* dressing to keep out air, or use the inside of a *clean* handkerchief or pillow case. Do not use fluffy cloth. If your patient is awake, give him sips of cold water to replace fluid lost.

**DON'T**

Don't touch the injury, or even breathe on it.

Don't pull off burnt cloth.

Don't burst blisters.

Don't put on cream or ointment.

27

## CLOTHES ON FIRE

It is natural for someone to run away from fire, but if his clothes are burning, running will only make the flames worse. The faster the person runs, the bigger the flames will become and the worse the burn will be. Fire spreads upwards, so the flames could reach the face.

HEAT
AIR
INFLAMMABLE
MATERIAL

The fire triangle shows the three things needed to keep a fire burning. Removing one of them will break the triangle and put out the fire.

**Action**

**Stop your patient from running. Pull him down on to the ground as quickly as you can, with the burning area on top.**

If water is available, pour it directly on to the place where the clothes are actually burning, not on to the flames, as they are above the seat of the fire.

If water is not available, smother the flames with a blanket, coat or rug. Beat on the blanket with your hands to put out the flames. Don't roll your patient over and over under the blanket. This might only spread the flames around his body. When approaching your patient take care to hold the blanket in front of you for your own safety.

**DON'T**

Don't use nylon cloth to smother the flames – this shrivels and melts in heat.

## ABOUT THE BODY
## 4 THE SKELETON

The body is built round a framework of bones called the skeleton. Bones give shape to the body, and protect it from injury. They also act as levers for the muscles to pull against.

Some bones are joined together and cannot move. Those in the skull form a strong box to keep the brain safe from bumps and falls. Other bones can move only slightly. The spine or backbone is actually a column of 33 bones linked together with discs, which allow some movement and act as shock absorbers. The spine keeps the body upright and contains a tunnel which protects the vital spinal cord. From the spine, twelve pairs of ribs form a cage round the chest to protect the heart and lungs.

### Joints

Movable bones meet at a joint, which is protected by an elastic bag filled with fluid to "oil" the moving ends. This prevents wear and tear. Some joints, such as those at the elbow and knee, can bend in only one direction, like a hinge. Others are more flexible and can swivel. The shoulder and hip are examples of this kind of "ball and socket" joint.

### Fractures

Bones may be fractured (broken) by a direct blow. Sometimes the force of a sudden blow travels along the bones, and causes a break elsewhere. If you fall heavily on your outstretched hand, for instance, the shock may travel up your arm and break the collarbone, in front of your shoulder.

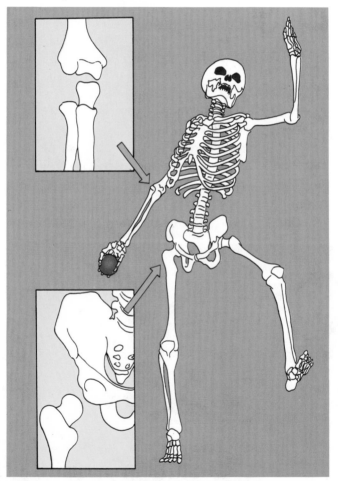

## BROKEN BONES

It is important to prevent a broken bone from being moved. If it is, the jagged end can very easily cause more serious injury.

It is often difficult to decide whether an injured bone is broken or pushed out of place, or the joint strained. The First Aid you give is the same.

Your patient will be in great pain, especially if he tries to move the injured part, or if the injury is touched. The flesh round it will be swollen and, if the injury is in an arm or leg, the limb might lie in a strange position. It will not look right.

### Action
1 **Don't move the patient. Warn him to keep still.**

2 Carefully place padding, such as a pillow or rolled-up coat, against each side of the injury to protect it from movement.
3 Cover your patient with a coat or blanket to keep him warm.
4 Fetch a grown-up.

Sometimes when a bone breaks there is also bleeding. You might even see bone in the wound. Don't be alarmed. Cover the wound gently with a dressing, but don't press on it. If blood is spurting or pouring out, press *alongside* the broken bone to bring the edges of the wound together, but take care not to move the injury.

**DON'T**
Don't give anything to eat or drink.

## GETTING HELP

When you have given immediate First Aid, your next important duty is to get a grown-up to help. Any grown-up you see will usually come if you tell them something is wrong.

If no one is about, run to the nearest house or shop for help.

DIALLING 999

You may have to telephone for help from a public call-box. You don't need money to make an emergency call. Just pick up the receiver and dial 999. The operator will ask you which emergency service you require. Say "ambulance" and wait. When you are connected with the ambulance service, talk slowly and clearly. Explain where the accident is and what has happened. Don't put the telephone down until your message has been repeated back to you. Some people are so upset that they forget to pass on an important part of the message. Then they hang up before they can be asked for more information.

*Dialling 999 in the dark*

1 Find the telephone dial with your fingers. Feel down the right-hand side of the dial until you come to the finger stop near the bottom.

2 The hole just past this is the figure '0'. Put your second finger into this.

3 Put your first finger into the hole to the left of the '0'. This is the '9'.

4 Dial the '9' three times by repeating these actions, without taking your finger out of the hole!

**DON'T**

Don't dial 999 unless there is an emergency. Some foolish people call out an ambulance when no one has been hurt. Then it isn't available to send to a real accident.

## MAKING YOUR PATIENT COMFORTABLE

Shock is not just a bad fright. It is a word doctors use to describe how the body reacts to an accident, especially if there has been bad bleeding or severe burns.

Someone suffering from shock *looks* ill. His face is pale and his skin feels cold and sweaty. He may be dizzy or sick. His breathing becomes faster and weaker, and he may even become unconscious.

You must always do your best to make your patient comfortable. This helps to lessen the effects of shock.

**Action**

**Lay your patient on a rug or blanket. Place him on his back, with his head low and turned to one side. Loosen tight clothing round his neck, chest or waist.**

Raise his legs so that blood will flow back into his brain. If he has a head, chest or stomach injury he may feel more comfortable half sitting up with his head and shoulders supported.

Cover him with a coat or blanket to keep him warm, but not too hot. Shelter him from wind or rain. Hot sun is harmful so you may have to make some kind of shade.

If he feels thirsty, moisten his lips with a wet cloth. Should he feel sick, or become unconscious, place him in the Recovery Position. *(See page 12.)*

KEEP CALM

Anyone who has had a bad accident will feel frightened. Keep calm. Tell your patient what you are doing to help. Talk to him while you are waiting for a doctor or an ambulance. Sometimes all you will need to do is hold his hand.

## STINGS

A sting from an insect, jellyfish or plant usually causes only redness and slight swelling round the sting, with some pain or itching.

**Action**

Scrape off the sting poison sac, if it has been left in the skin. Don't pull it off as this will squeeze more poison in. Treat with antihistamine cream right away, or cool with calamine lotion or a cold compress.

A sting inside the mouth is more dangerous, because the throat might swell up and make breathing difficult. If this happens, place your patient in the Recovery Position. *(See page 12.)* Give him sips of cold water or an ice cube to suck, and place a cold, wet cloth against the neck to reduce swelling. Get help as quickly as possible.

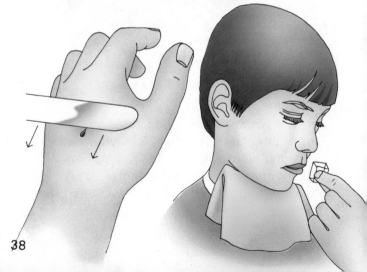

## ANIMAL BITES

Animal bites are always dangerous, even if they do not look serious. Animals' mouths are full of germs and their sharp, pointed teeth can bite deeply, causing infection.

### Action

**Wash, *away* from the bite, with warm, soapy water or antiseptic solution, cover with a dressing, and take your patient to a doctor.**

## BLISTERS

A blister is caused by rough material rubbing against the skin. It forms when the surface of the skin is separated from the inner layers and becomes a bubble filled with fluid called plasma. This protects the new skin being formed underneath. New or badly fitting shoes are a common cause.

### Action

**Cover the blister with a gauze dressing or adhesive plaster.**

### DON'T

Don't prick or squeeze the blister as this might let dirt and germs into the new skin.

## GRIT IN THE EYE

The eye is very delicate and should not be rubbed or interfered with. The eye protects itself from damage by making tears to wash away specks of dirt or tiny insects which may become trapped on the surface of the eye, or under the eyelid.

### Action

**Blinking rapidly will often produce enough tears to wash away any irritation. If this doesn't work, you may be able to wash out the eye with some wet cotton wool, or with an eye-bath or eggcupful of water.**

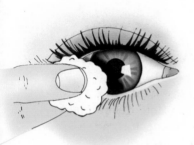

*Fill eye-bath two-thirds full. Lean forward and place eye-bath over whole of eye. Move head from side to side with eye open to wash out foreign body*

### DON'T

Don't rub or touch the eye as this could very easily make an injury much worse. If you can't clear the irritation, close the eyelids and cover the eye with a gauze dressing or pad of cotton wool. Take your patient to a grown-up or a doctor.

## SPLINTERS AND THORNS

Wood splinters and thorns, especially in the finger or knee, may be very painful, but are usually removed quite easily.

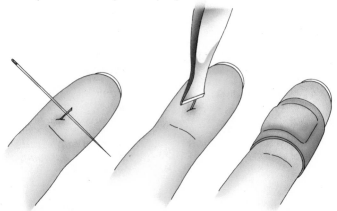

### Action

If one end of the splinter is still above the surface of the skin, prise it upwards with a needle which has been wiped with cotton wool soaked in antiseptic solution. Remove with tweezers. The splinter may be reached more easily if the skin around it is gently squeezed between finger and thumb.

As most small splinters usually work themselves out in time, they are sometimes best left alone. If a splinter cannot be easily removed, wipe the skin around it with antiseptic solution and cover with a small adhesive plaster. Ask for grown-up help.

# A HANDY FIRST AID KIT

It's a good idea to have your own First Aid Kit to use at home, in the car, or to take on an outing. Here are the most useful items to include, with their uses.

| *CONTENTS* | *USE FOR . . .* |
| --- | --- |
| **2 large wound dressings** | *. . . covering large wounds or burns.* |
| **2 packets of gauze dressings** | *. . . pads or swabs; covering small wounds or burns.* |
| **Small packet of cotton wool** | *. . . cleaning minor cuts or grazes; applying ointments or solutions.* |
| **2 triangular bandages** | *. . . keeping dressings in place; supporting injured limbs; pads or dressings; cold compresses.* |
| **2 open-wove bandages** | *. . . keeping dressings in place.* |
| **Crepe bandage** | *. . . keeping dressings in place; supporting minor strains.* |
| **Bottle of antiseptic solution** | *. . . cleaning dirt from minor cuts or grazes (dilute according to instructions on the bottle).* |
| **Tube of antiseptic cream** | *. . . treating minor cuts or grazes.* |

| **Tube of antihistamine cream** | *. . . treating stings.* |
| **Bottle of calamine lotion** | *. . . cooling stings or sunburn.* |
| **Box of adhesive plasters** | *. . . covering minor cuts, grazes, stings or blisters.* |
| **Roll of adhesive tape** | *. . . keeping bandages or dressings in place.* |
| **Tweezers** | *. . . removing thorns or splinters.* |
| **Scissors** | *. . . cutting bandages or tape, removing clothing.* |
| **Safety pins** | *. . . pinning bandages in place.* |

Keep these items clean, in a waterproof container. Dressings, cotton wool and bandages should be kept clean in sealed packets until used. Before using your First Aid Kit, remember to wash your hands thoroughly in warm, soapy water.

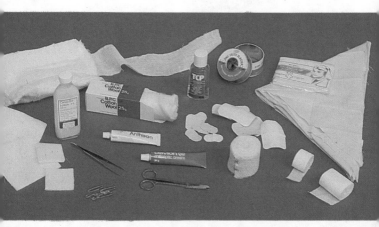

## DRESSINGS AND BANDAGES

A *dressing* is a piece of gauze cloth. It is used to cover a wound to keep it clean and help stop bleeding. It should be large enough to cover the wound completely. When applying a dressing you must take great care to keep it clean. Hold it only by the corners and don't lay it down. A dressing can be held in place with a bandage or adhesive tape.

There are three kinds of bandages:

### The triangular bandage

This has many different uses. It can be made into a sling to support an injured arm, or folded as an ordinary bandage. It may also be used as a pad to stop bleeding or as a cold compress.

Two triangular bandages are made by cutting a metre square of linen or calico cloth diagonally in half.

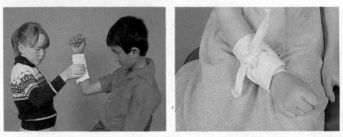

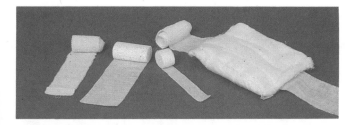

### The roller bandage

This may be made of cotton or elasticated crepe. It is available in different widths for use on various parts of the body. The roller bandage is used to keep dressings in place, or support a strain or bruise.

A specially prepared roller bandage called a *wound dressing* can be applied quickly and easily. It has a sterile dressing and cotton wool pad already attached near one end.

### The tubular bandage

This is quicker and easier to use, especially on fingers. It is a roll of gauze tubing, and is applied with the help of a specially designed applicator, which slips it easily on to the finger.

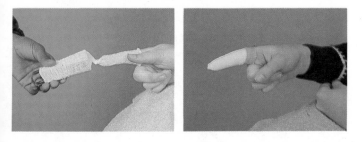

## FOLDING TRIANGULAR BANDAGES

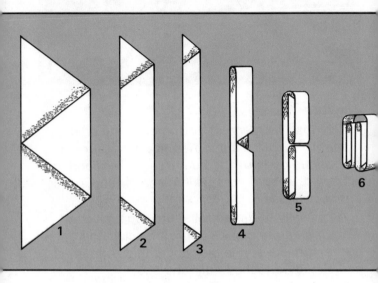

1 Fold point across to base.

2 Fold in half again to make a broad bandage.

3 Fold in half again to make a narrow bandage.

4 When the bandage is not in use, make a narrow bandage, then fold the ends into the middle.

5 Fold the ends a second time.

6 Fold in half and seal in a packet to keep it clean.

## ARM SLING

The *arm sling* is used to support an injured arm. Hold bandage with the point towards your patient's injured arm and one end towards his other shoulder. Turn the end behind his neck and bring it forward over the shoulder on the injured side. Pad the arm for protection and gently place it across the bandage, with hand held higher than the elbow. Lift the lower end up over the arm and tie both ends together in front of the shoulder with a reef knot. Finish by folding the point forward over the elbow, tucking it in neatly and fastening it with a safety pin. You should still be able to see your patient's fingertips.

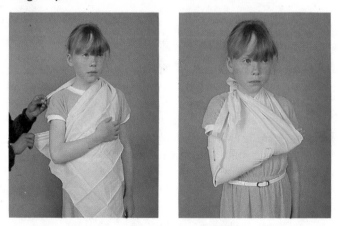

When tying a reef knot, which is flat and easily untied, remember to tie the ends left over right, right over left.

## TRIANGULAR SLING

A *triangular sling* serves a different purpose from an arm sling. It is used to support an injured hand or forearm, by holding the hand high to stop bleeding and ease pain. Gently place the injured arm across the chest, with the fingers up in front of the opposite shoulder. Cover the injured arm with the triangular bandage, holding one end up to the shoulder above the injured hand, the point over the elbow of the injured arm, and leaving the other end hanging down.

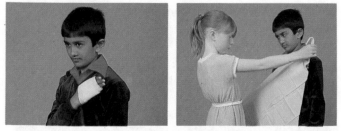

Gently tuck the base of the bandage up between the injured arm and the chest, making the sling. Twist the bandage round two or three times just below the elbow, then carry the lower end round the patient's back and bring it over the opposite shoulder. Tie the two ends together with a reef knot just above the injured hand.

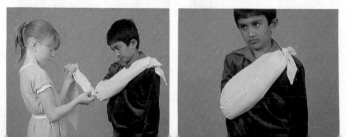

## RING PAD

Sometimes it isn't possible to press directly on to a wound to stop bleeding. There may be glass in it, or a bone may be broken. A *ring pad* made from a narrow bandage will keep a dressing in place without disturbing the wound.

To make a ring pad, hold one end of a narrow bandage between the finger and thumb of one hand, and wind it round the fingers several times.

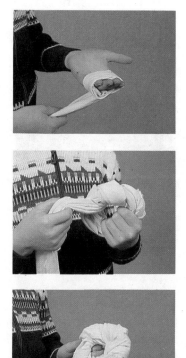

Remove the bandage from your fingers and twist the remainder of the bandage tightly in and out of the hole, gradually working round the circle.

Keep the ring pad in place over the wound by using another triangular bandage as either a narrow or broad bandage.

## ROLLER BANDAGES

When applying a *roller bandage* don't unroll more than about 15 cms at a time, and be careful not to let it fall and unroll completely. Apply with the bandage roll on the side of the bandage away from the limb being bandaged.

The bandage must be firm enough to hold the dressing in place, but not so tight that it stops the circulation of the blood. Leave finger tips

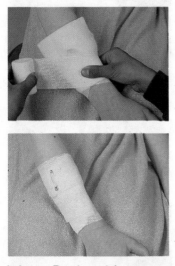

and toes unbandaged so that you can check the circulation. If the bandage is too tight, they will feel cold and turn bluish.

*For arm or leg*
Support the injured arm or leg in a comfortable position so that it can be bandaged without having to be moved. Start from below an

injury. Begin with one complete turn round the limb to hold the bandage in position, then firmly but gently bandage upwards and over the injury. With each turn, cover about two-thirds of the previous turn. Finish off the bandage above the injury with another complete turn and keep it in

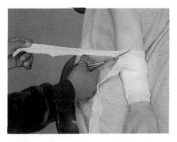

place with a safety pin or adhesive tape, or tie with a reef knot. To finish a bandage with a knot, cut the end in half several centimetres up its length. Tie at end of cut with a simple overhand knot. Pass the two ends round the limb in opposite directions, and tie with a reef knot.

*For a joint*

Support the elbow, knee or heel in a comfortable position. Start bandaging with one complete turn round the widest part of the joint. Firmly wind the bandage round the limb alternately above and below the joint. With each turn, cover about two-thirds of the previous turn.

Cut the end of the bandage and finish off with a reef knot, or fasten with a safety pin *(see above or opposite)*.

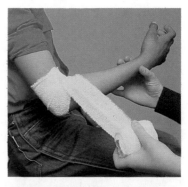

# INDEX